T0166499

SMOKE SHOW

SMOKE SHOW

A NOVEL BY
CLINT BURNHAM

ARSENAL PULP PRESS

Vancouver

SMOKE SHOW
Copyright © 2005 by Clint Burnham

ARSENAL PULP PRESS
341 Water Street, Suite 200
Vancouver, BC, Canada, V6B 1B8
arsenalpulp.com

The publisher gratefully acknowledges the support of the Canada Council for the Arts and the British Columbia Arts Council for its publishing program, and the Government of Canada through the Book Publishing Industry Development Program for its publishing activities.

This is a work of fiction. Any resemblance of characters to persons either living or deceased is purely coincidental.

Printed and bound in Canada

Library and Archives Canada Cataloguing in Publication

Burnham, Clint, 1962-
Smoke show / Clint Burnham.
ISBN 1-55152-196-2
I. Title.
PS8553.U665S66 2005   C813'.54   C2005-903966-3
ISBN-13 978-155152-196-1

Design by Tim Lee

FOR JULIE, WHO FOUND IT

SMOKE SHOW

GOING DOWNTOWN. Dream date.

How long did you get the babysitter.

Schoolgirl look: she wore tartan socks, short skirt, lots of makeup.

She had a gauze bandage on her hand.

Let's get off and get a coupla sacks of bennies. Romeo plotting seduction.

Hey how come you have pimples still if you're twenty-three? How come you still got pimples on your face if you're twenty-three? He had blond hair, thin to his skull like Kevin Costner's in *Waterworld*. He was talking to the woman in front of him.

How come you got pimples on your dick? The two P'ilipina girls laughed.

I don't have herpes if that's what you think.

Bye, pimple dick!

Do you know him? Well, he sure knows you.

Guy talked to his girl. She was sitting.

Was your hand bleeding when you –

Yeah well you know I was.

You know, cuz I was.

Yeah, well I was trying to get Julian, watching him when –

Someone had a Walkman, playing bhangra or filmi music –

Cuz you know so there was like blood just flying through the air?. . . we saw it I saw it goin' from the –

And then I was on the phone.

So you were like bleeding on the phone?

She looked away, down at the floor.

He wore tight black Wranglers, boots with silver, a mauve silk shirt, the hem saggin'. Was your hand bleeding when you were on the phone?

I don't know, was yours? She glared at him quick. Yeah, like –

Were, cuz –

Yeah, I told you I was turning around for Julian.

He had scars on his arms. Yeah cuz there was blood flying. . . .

EAN/UPC/Title   **Batch 509**   **2 A**

9/05/2006
10:19:19

Quantity
1

9781551521961

Title
SMOKE SHOW

Title#   Pub – Item#   Category
008276997   **QP**

Author
BURNHAM CLINT   Unit ID

PO Number
000406011

Cell ID
3CELL011A   * U   D34326262 *

And I was, went to the phone.

Yeah cuz you know, huh the blood just flew through the air?

THE RADIO WAS ON LATE AT NIGHT. How was that?

Jimmy at their place, Jimmy and Lucy's house of crack. East Van, trees on the streets, little houses for sale.

Jimmy was wondering.

Oh yeah well you know like, umm, yeah, well, you know like whatevah, umm, so like you know, so like what's up with them? I mean like it – like it's – ah they're pretty neat, I'm amazed at how much people, you know, go to the effort.

Well, this is the name for them. They were sitting in their living room, the entertainment centre.

What was that one I smelled the other night, reminded me of my grandparents' place?

Boxwood.

Yeah. Yeah. Boxwood. Man, when I get that smell, I don't know, it's like hedge city, I can just remember, I don't know. He sprawled on the chair. What's in – what's interesting is they're not solid. They're one of those things where they look solid but they're not.

Yeah, good, with ya so far.

No cuz you know cuz they're just trimmed, right? I mean, they don't grow as these big square or whatever things.

Brilliant. Stop the presses.

No just wait. So –

When, we were kids, when we'd go walking with my dad, he'd throw us in hedges. Yeah, he'd just suddenly push us into a hedge.

Did you like it?

Oh, we loved it. Are you kidding? A chance to tear clothing? Don't pass it up. Mandatory.

So what are hedges then? Why're they there?

Oh c'mon. Figure it out on your own time.

Yeah but he's like doing this math, you wouldn't believe it.

Yeah, but it's just cuz he's our friend that we can even get it from him, right? I mean, that was almost all he had left. Jimmy defends the honour of Randy, otherwise not present. They're sitting around.

Oh sure, yeah. So what do you mean. Jennifer sipped her tea. Oh, tastes gross.

Yeah, eh? At least it's not your piss.

She took a gulp, pushed a cheek up into her squinting eye. Guess so.

Din' you hear that? If you, you can recycle your piss when you take shrooms or whatever, hallucinogenics. Or the one in mushrooms, anyway.

Oh yeah? She said it like an Ozzie, yee-uh?

Yeah like it stays active.

Yeah, did you see them like spray their piss out into outer space?

Oh really?

Gross.

Yeah.

What was it, where did they do that?

On that show.

No, what show was that?

Oh, that one, the one about the astronauts.

The computer one?

Yeah.

Jimmy got up and went into the bedroom.

Oh, is he getting the stuff.

Hunh, no, it's in the fridge.

He came back out with a CD.

So what're you puttin' on there, Lucy asked. More metal?

Yeah, you got a problem?

No, go ahead. I just thought if we're going to get fucked up.

Yeah Jimmy, get something kind of spacey. Something reeeally sloow and trance-y.

Let's get fucked *up*.

SO WHAT, D'YOU THINK WE SHOULD GO TO CRAPPY TIRE. Jimmy engages right after, should we buy s'more lube?

Yeah. Guess so. If I don't get claustrophobic, with those shelves.

Yeah I know.

Yeah, get some plastic stuff made by Chinese slaves.

A bucket.

A bucket, guess I better get a mop.

Yeah, and I want to get one of those croquet sets.

He pushed himself up from the broke-back easy chair. Anything else we should get?

No. I've been spending too much money lately. I can't afford this.

Do you want to roll it here? Ray and Jimmy walked into the kitchen.

Yeah, it's great.

You know, I thought, with the baby.

Oh yeah, no, she's cool. She's too young to know.

Yeah.

But, you know, once I took in a roach clip of my mom's for show and tell?

Nnn-oo!

Oh yeah.

Did she know?

No, I mean no, she didn't know I was going to. So I'm there, and it's show and tell, and I whip it out, this clip, it was one of those feathered ones, you know, like you can get on Hornby Island or at the Renaissance Faire back in the day.

Hil-*ar*-ious.

Yeah, she was a real hippie. So I'm like, this is a roach clip and my mom uses it to smoke grass.

Oh no.

Oh yeah.

So like, did they pay your mom a visit?

Oh yeah. There was a little conference.

IN A JAMAICAN RESTAURANT, SHE WATCHED THE TV BEHIND HIM. A fucking car chase, 60 mph and neutral. Oil pressure up: billowing dust, Dennis Weaver (McLeod's? that's the store, *McCloud?*) looking half-crazed at the car's gauges. She was going to check the TV listings at home but forgot. Maybe it was the cowboy cop one with him.

THE CHANNEL CHANGED AND IT WAS THE GUY IN A BACKYARD, POINTING AT THE SKY.

I DON'T KNOW, I JUST DON'T LIKE IT WHEN, YOU KNOW, THEY GET TOO MUCH ON THE GUITAR. That's why I don't like that Jeff Healey. Well, that's about it. Tom walked to the back of the truck, took a look inside. He climbed down off the tailgate.

No, you gotta check for plants.

Yeah.

Yeah, and don't forget Spot.

Yeah, that'd be it, eh? Don't think I could live that one down.

YEAH, SO LIKE I HAD A DREAM ABOUT HIM, EH? Oh yeah, the other night. Amazing. God, he's just –

AND YOU KNOW COLIN, COLIN JAMES – THERE – HE'S REAL VERSATILE, EH? He'll do the jazz and the big band, and now it's the soul. Tom liked to talk about music.

Yeah, he keeps inventing himself. Well, you know they've got a really good thing happening in terms of these artists there, they're running, and that just doesn't happen with – Jimmy heard someone say that.

Yeah.

So, like are you working lots of overtime?

Oh no, it's just this training I have to go in for. You know, and I get what? Double and a half, and by the time they've taken off your taxes at their end, really, I'd rather have the day off, you know what I mean? But that's the life of the blue collar worker. I don't know, I'm bored there. Wearing out the back of my boots. So anyway, here, let's get these out. You want gloves? Cuz I've got them.

THEY GOT UP AND JIMMY WAS THINKING ABOUT SMOKING A JOINT AFTER BREAKFAST. He had cereal and pushed it around, building forts, clearings in the rough bush.

OK. So d'you want to go downtown this morning? She came out putting on an earring, her head tilted to one side.

I guess we could do that.

Take the bus.

Yeah.

He took out the Ziploc bag of dope. Did you dry much last night?

Huh, no. She was in the bathroom.

He walked into the kitchen with the bag. Miked it up, singing *funky on the mike*, smelling the fumes.

OK. I love that.

Pooh, I don't know. Yeah I *know* what it smells like. He held the bag under her face as she tried to put on mascara. Get away.

He went back out and rolled a joint. She came out and they sat next to each other on the chesterfield. She took a drag. Pooh – man, this stuff's killer.

Yeah, potent, eh?

They passed it around a couple more times and she went That's enough for me, thanks.

OK so let's get going.

Yeah right. OK, no hurry.

Alright. You got any bus tickets?

Yeah.

'K.

The bus was crowded when they got on. Downtown, they could hear the race cars. It's the Indy, it's the Indy, she jumped up and down.

JEFF WAS IN THE POOL. Hey, so like you should be able to sell some around here with these guys moving in, eh? Just –

Yeah, I'll go around with my card and like get listings.

Yeah just go. Did you see those new people moved in? First day and they're par-*ty*-ing. He had himself up on the edge on his elbow, drinking from a can of PC Dry.

Tom walked over and sat down. He took a long pull of beer. Jeez, you know, usually it's me who's the first one in the pool.

We can fix that. They grabbed him to throw him in. He didn't struggle much. Just a sec, Jeff went, let me get his wallet out.

Aw fuck that, but he got it out and put it on the plastic white table.

Tom's dad had his arms and said, On three. They threw him in and he came up, his hair flat against his skull, mouth like a fish, eyes wide open. He pulled himself out of the pool. Jesus, that's not bad. After all that, I tell you. He made a grab for Jennifer and she pulled back.

No way. Nope. I've got my watch on. Don't.

Aw, that's no excuse. One of her girlfriends made to give her a push too.

No, I know, I bought 'er it, I should know.

Aw, but your mistake was to ask her eh?

Yep, remember girls, No means yes! No means yes!

Yep, you can't win.

But he walked back to the house. Man, this shirt's like a tarp when it's wet.

Jeff cupped his hands. Yeah, so Tom, we're just going to do a smoke show out front eh?

Hey I don't care.

Oh yeah, just party on your front lawn. Maybe rip up some turf?

Yeah, Trev'll be out there and I'll just lay this patch. A fuckin' Pun burn, fuckin' stand on the brake and just lay 'er.

OK SO LET'S CHECK LONDON DRUGS FIRST. They usually. Jimmy and Lucy were on a consumer mission.

Yeah, OK. I have to get some batteries anyway.

So like, there's these test hedges, eh, that they grow. Jimmy had an obsession.

What?

Test hedges. Some have been growing for more than a century at experimental farms.

Just like in the Big Little Books!

Yeah?

Yeah yeah. Don't you remember? They had those adventures with the cat, Tom, or Bugs Bunny. And they were at the laboratories, right, and had scientists.

Yeah.

Yeah, and I never, I couldn't figure out what a scientist was. It was like they were always weird.

Yeah OK. I'm with ya.

So –

So?

The hedges!

I'VE GOT TO BE CAREFUL. Jimmy says he has to be careful. I didn't pay for the film.

No? Lucy appeared unconcerned. She could care less.

No, I just had it, and I stuck it in my pocket when we left. Didn't even think about it.

Yeah, that happens.

Better be careful though. They don't see it that way.

Yeah OK. OK, are we going in here?

Yep. She put on her *Star Trek* voice. Prepare for mall entry. They were both wearing sunglasses.

Jesus, so much space. Jimmy had a mild condition of agoraphobia. The department store was a perfumed barn, with linoleum and carpet instead of dirt, yuppies with goatees instead of hicks in foam and net hats.

I can't believe how much they spread out the stuff here, what's the point? Doesn't make the shit any better.

No. Let's get through to the mall. Which way, this way? Lucy led the way. Their saviour. They made it out of the store, into the mall.

Tom stopped in front of him and got out of the pick-up. He stuck a can of Kokanee in the window. Road pop.

Jeff pushed the gears around and took 99 across to Ladner. People were on the lawn of Tom and Jen's new place and trucks were parked everywhere. They got the stuff out and then sat around the pool. After the grandparents left, Jen asked who wanted to smoke a joint with her.

Me. He was pushing buttons on the blaster.

Uh oh. Sounds like the batteries're gone.

So what're you going to do, Jesse asked Jen. They stood around the porch, leaning on the railings, passing around the joint. Jen started a second one and a couple of them kept the last of the roach going between them.

Give it to the birds, feed the birds. Richler's drunken birds, eating rotten apples.

Hey, not in the yard?

What, oh yeah, fuck it. Sure. Some bird'll find it and it'll make his day. You know, like, whoa. Tom was expansive with his arm gestures, in a curious way, as if he were wearing a life jacket.

So this is pretty good, eh?

So what're you guys gonna do?

Oh not much.

But everyone wants some tea, eh?

Oh yeah, for sure.

Jen, you want some?

Oh yeah.

You sure?

Yeah.

So Jimmy, you think, maybe I could get like ten hits from you?

Yeah, sure.

So like, how much. Blowing on the tea, he took a sip.

Oh, just what we paid for it.

Cool.

Yeah, we don't –

Yeah, so we paid, umm, well a buck a piece, I think it was like 28 bucks, I don't know.

Yeah, you shoulda seen Randy, he's doing all this math.

Total stoner, eh?

No, he's actually together.

Well.

No, he is, I mean, he has these projects all the time.

YEAH, SO LIKE I GUESS I'M MOSTLY CLASSIC ROCK.

HE WAS CUTTING UP SOME WIENERS. He grabbed a cup for the kid.

HEY, SO JEEZ YOU GUYS GOT A GREAT PLACE, EH?

Yeah, we like it, I like it.

Yeah, well, pretty lucky. Oh, right on. Where'd you find *that?*

On the street.

No way.

So're you getting money from the air force? Jimmy and Ray are in the kitchen. Still.

No, they got rid of me. There was this girl I was seeing and they set me up.

No way, I know this guy –

And you know what was really ironic was that it was her dad I was smoking with. You know –

Was he in the service too?

What? No, I wouldn't, you know, tell them, finger him.

Oh no, I didn't –

You know and they wanted me to, though, you know I could have, but no way, I'm not gonna. No, they wanted me to, you know, tell them, and I'm like No way.

Oh yeah, no, you can't, I wouldn't. No yeah, they're, that's fucked.

So like what you're – You need some scissors? Jimmy asked Ray.

No, I chop it up in the coffee grinder. You ever done that? It's great, all fine and small.

He stood in the kitchen rolling one. The kid was in the other room with Lucy and Jesse. They were talking about men. Or Jesse was.

Yeah, but so like he was like, all this time he's had this crush on me. And it's a drag, and his cousin was there and she says to me in the bathroom, what are you doing with my cousin.

So what d'you want to do? Smoke in here or outside?

No, we should go outside. Not with the kid.

They walked into the living room. Hey Jesse, d'you want a beer?

No, it's not twelve yet. Oh jeez, I better change him. I have to go out to the car.

Yeah, OK. Ray tossed her the keys. Make sure you lock it, eh?

Yeah yeah.

YEAH, SO HOW LONG D'YOU THINK HE'LL LAST IN THERE – HE WON'T LAST LONG. Ray wanted to talk about the trial.

Oh yeah, he's not going to be in protective, eh?

They walked outside and Jimmy lit the joint.

Yeah, they'll just like rip him.

They're putting – he's going to work in wood shop. Yeah right. For about five minutes. That's stupid.

Well, they'll take care of him. Yeah but cuz like they go for the sickos, eh? Cuz that's even too far for them.

Oh great, that doesn't mean anything. It'll just be *another* sicko who kills him.

Yeah well why should we pay?

THEY STOOD OUTSIDE SMOKING, THE KID WANDERING IN THE GARDEN PULLING UP PLANTS.

So, like you guys have a clothesline, eh?

Yeah don't tell anyone. I'm going to rip it out, I hate it. I'm lazy.

Yeah, we'll –

So we'll have to get you out there.

What? Oh yeah. Definitely.

BUT NOW ANYONE CAN HAVE A HEDGE. Or you see them everywhere, anyway.

No, you need the money and the time. Hedge money, hedge fund.

Oh! He chuckled. Yeah well with electric clippers, it's like easy. Not like before, with only the real clippers. Then you worked at it.

Hey, you've got pussy breath.

I guess I do. Yeah? He kissed her again. Problem?

No, I enjoyed that.

Radio Shack's fucking insane, they've got $200 answering machines. We should just get that one at the drugstore. They don't have any that cheap.

OK, sure.

On the bus, on the way home, they saw guys at the Ivanhoe watching the Indy trials, standing on the roof with binoculars.

THEY GOT OUT OF THE VAN AND RAY STAYED BEHIND WITH THE KID.

I'm going to get something to eat, Jesse said.

OK.

Jimmy took a piss, tucking his dick back into his trunks under his cut-offs. Piss dripped down his leg as he walked. He kept thinking he could smell it, but everyone was eating food. No one noticed.

THEY DROVE TO JERICHO BEACH AND FOUND A GOOD SPOT. Jimmy got the beers out of the stroller and put them in the shade, opening one. Lucy had the ciders in her bag. They took them out. Ray took out a joint from his pocket.

You guys are sure you didn't see her hat, eh?

Nope.

I wonder where it coulda gotten to.

I don't know.

They got some food going on a blanket, slicing open buns, putting ham on them, cheese. OK, so like dig in, folks. Time for grub. Jesse pulled Sarah over, sat her on her lap on the grass and gave her a quarter sandwich.

They sunned themselves, smoking and drinking.

Yeah, so that's pretty gross about Mary, eh?

No, what happened?

Lucy, do you know Mary? My friend from Victoria? Well, anyways she was going to this new doctor, eh? Up in the Valley, and he's, she's going to him for her knee. Cuz you know it got fucked up in that car accident she had. And she was going to this one doctor but then she moved to Comox, eh? So she gets this new one and everything's going great, and then all of a sudden it turns out he's been like, you know like feeling her up and everything! Gross, huh? Ooh, if some doctor did that to me I'd just like, get outta there. You know. I mean like, can you imagine? Her eyes narrowed as she pulled on the cigarette.

She laughed deeply. Yeah, so like, I'm quitting next week, when I start school. For sure.

Oh wow, go for it. Lucy was impressed with her resolve. She'd never quit anything.

Yeah, well I'm, I may as well. I mean yeah, stress, whatever, but I just can't afford it. With what welfare's giving me, you know, I move into a cheaper place to save money and they cut back my payment. You know – six-fifty after rent now. I can't live on that. Not with the kid. I've gotta do something. You know, maybe make something and sell it, or work for someone UT, y'know, under the table.

Oh yeah, I mean like.

It's crazy, eh?

Yeah, it's like crazy they expect you to live on that.

So what do you think of me moving over here, eh?

Oh yeah, that'd be great.

Yeah, well, when I, I remember when I told Dave that I was moving up to the Valley he was like oh no! Not, you know, he was, you know, he wasn't totally supportive. But I just had to get away. I just had to, you know it's such a switch from living with different people, and trying to get the money for the rent, and now it just comes offa my welfare cheque so I don't have to worry. You know like instead of before. But it was just too, now I'm hoping I'll – I need to focus. I really have to do that.

JIMMY READ SOME MAIL AS HE LISTENED TO BIG BLACK.

> . . . a couple of days ago in Toronto's best resource centre, the subway. Serendipity and commuter detouring due to the TTC disaster found me on the opposite side of the tracks from Alex and Paul at the Spadina subway station. We had a good five minute chat (OK, five minute shout) (Jim lost his what? His virtue . . . ? Oh, his furniture) without even receiving too many hostile looks . OK – I was wearing a long black summer dress and a black straw hat . . . who could be hostile? (Alex and Paul looked beautiful . . .)

He went and got a bottle of beer and tried to open it on his T-shirt hem, but it wasn't a twist-off, so he got out the church key.

> Alex and Paul look beautiful. Jim lost his what? Did I tell you it's very hot here . . . I'm a tiny mongoose, running from the heat . . . No, actually – I'm sitting on my fire escape next to a tree that recently had one of its branches cut off for the offense of rubbing against the evestrough. On the stump of the tree, twenty-odd feet above the ground, have gathered all sorts of different insects, like the usually antagonistic-towards-each-other animals at the pond fleeing from the fire. They are obviously attracted to the sap. Or to me. I'm the sap. There's a large bee/wasp with white markings that looks like a police helicopter, ants ranging from miniature to B movie, bees, and the most incredible butterfly that, when it folds up its wings, looks like a desiccated autumn leaf.

> You're probably tired of this rhapsody on Nature, but S has gone to Calgary for 12 days, and Nature is as close to sex as I'm going to get.

WHAT I'LL DO IS IF I'M BY MYSELF, I'LL JUST LIKE ROLL A JOINT, AND ONLY LIKE SMOKE THE FIRST LIKE YOU KNOW JUST OVER HALF. And then leave it and then come back to it later, you know, so you don't have to like roll one right away.

HE READ IN THE PAPER ABOUT THEME RESTAURANTS AND, ON A MORE SERIOUS NOTE, BROADWAY.

YEAH, BUT PEOPLE DON'T USUALLY HAVE IT.

Yeah, I know what you mean.

Like, they don't usually have it that, you know, worked out.

Worked out, yeah. The sound of a truck backing up, or a microwave done.

HEY HOW'RE YOU DOIN'? OK eh?

Yeah. Yeah.

Yeah OK, huh. Kernel. Yeah so OK. Hey, you want to open the window? Open the window, OK?

The white girl sitting up in front of him turned around, folding her legs under her. She pushed a couple of times on the window. Jeff got up and she opened the window. He sat back down again and continued abusing the guy next to him. That guy wore flip-up sunglasses and carried two plastic bags. He wore garden gloves. A cream windbreaker, and looked like the singer Jad Fair from the band Half Japanese.

So you want to get off now? Jeff talked to him. Get off, and, you know, go for it?

Uh, no.

Yeah OK so maybe we'll – this is your stop, eh? This your stop? So what're you doing? Going to the fireworks? So you know. Hey, so no one mind the rush from the window?

The guy shifted a bit on the seat, pushed his glasses up, the flip-up shades stuck to the light sheen on his forehead.

Yeah, so what if I had a gun, eh? You got a knife, no, you wouldn't carry a knife, don't have the guts. You wouldn't carry a knife, would you? Hey Howard.

The guy called Howard looked straight ahead, said no.

Yeah, knew that. So where you going? Going downtown? Going to

Waterworld? Gonna see it, eh? Some movie, eh? You seen it? Going
to *Waterworld*, fireworks? Yeah so you going to the fireworks? Not
much going on there. Something. Not much. So how's it going? Mind
if I, think I should fuck ya? Huh, you mind? Want me to shoot you?
Huh? Want that to happen? The bullet's bigger when it comes out, eh?
You know? Whole back of your head goes. So what're you going to,
Waterworld? You wanna sit here?

A little while later, a Native woman moved back in front of Jeff. He
got up and she sat down. Yeah good, so like I still wanna talk to my
buddy, eh? So how's it going, eh buddy? Yeah, want to keep an eye on
him. Don't want him getting away.

The woman looked at Jeff. Frowned then quickly smiled.

So where you going, where you going? Going home.

The girl who'd opened the window looked up at him. Nope.

Going to a movie? Yeah? What movie? *Waterworld?*

Umm, I don't know. Whatever. Some movie.

Yeah so, what movie? Don't you know? Don't you want to?

I don't really feel like having a conversation right now.

A guy across the aisle dropped some peanuts into his pocket and
stood up.

Hey, so what's up?

Not much.

Going to a movie?

Yeah. He smelled of gasoline.

Guys going together?

Yeah, you know.

Yeah, so what're you up to?

Oh you know, movie.

Yeah, so what're you seein'?

I don't know, *Glass Key. Glass* something.

Yeah, so what is it?

I don't know, some gangster movie.

White.

Yeah.

White gangster. Not a black one.

Yeah.

Yeah, so like, right on. You know, not *New Jack City*, hunh? *Boyz n the Hood.*

No, it's an old one. Black and white.

Yeah, same drug, different –

Same shit, different pile.

The woman at the back got up and Jeff sat down again. Hey let's talk some more, eh buddy? Get some talking, hey Jew-boy. Hey you better not report me to *The Buzzer*. So where you going? West End? Going to the West End? Huh? You like to go there.

No. The guy's jacket was zippered to his sternum.

Jeff kept putting his hand in his jacket pocket, poking with his finger. It was zipped up half-way: Body Glove.

Hey, you interested in our conversation? Pretty interesting, eh? Well, why don't you mind your own fucking business?

YEAH, WELL LIKE, SHE'S GREAT. Oh yeah, perfect person for me right now, eh? You know, cuz she's really focussed, eh? And you know, that's the perfect person for me. You know, cuz she's like. You know like. You know, I mean, the other day, she had to register her kid for this class and she like got up, and went there at, I don't know, before seven. I know it was before seven because I was up before seven with Sarah and she was gone then.

And mom and dad, they're like great. They're really really happy for me.

So like, when do you think Jess is going to show? Is she going to, she's not going to make it tonight, not now. She'll probably call or something.

He was hot and walked into the bedroom taking off his T-shirt. She was undressing and turned around. Her cunt was shaved, there was just a vertical line of bush. Her nipples were soft and erect. He pushed his pants off and scratched his balls, fluffing out the hair.

He rolled down onto the bed, pulling her down.

Hey, watch it, just take it easy.

He started kissing her on her belly and tits, then slowed down, kissing her on her shoulders and neck and face and lips. She kissed him back, and bit his shoulder and arm. She bit hard with sharp teeth and then pushed him off her, rolling onto him. She ground her clit against his cock and his belly, his hair.

She turned around so her ass was in his face and started stroking his cock. He pulled her hips down, and licked at her clit and lips. He moved his mouth around so he could lick all the way past her cunt, to her asshole. He stuck his tongue into her, pushing a bit. She was sucking hard on his dick, dragging her teeth into it. He licked from her asshole to her clit and back, and kept doing it, holding onto her hips and her ass, her knees spread outside his elbows.

She swung off him and lay on her front. Don't you want to whip me?

He took the small whip down off the wall and sat on her ass, his cock under her fist against her crack. He drew the whip gently on her back and then flicked it. She twitched a bit. He whipped her harder and she moved her ass around. She felt the hair on his balls between her cheeks and bit down on her lower lip, turning her face to the right.

HE SAT IN HIS BROTHER'S BEDROOM, SMOKING A JOINT, WATCHING THE OLD GUY ACROSS THE YARD PILE WOOD. He flipped through the brag book, looking at tight close-ups of an old duffer.

Before they were watching *Cops*. He used a remote with big rubber numbers.

Yeah, so we were at the bar, eh? And Jessica 'n me're there. We went dancing and there was all these guys, eh? Real, I dunno, creeps.

Huh, what were they?

Yeah, creeps, eh? She looked over at Lucy and laughed. These guys, she shuddered, all touching me. This one guy –

What were they, fishermen, cuz there wasn't any work so they were in the bar?

Her school when she was twelve or thirteen had its dances in the middle of the week so the loggers wouldn't crash it.

Yeah, he was a cop, eh?

D-ope.

Yeah, and he kept touching me. Yeah, so like. You know.

Well, he was a cop, so?

Yeah. He kept, you know. He was like putting his arms around me, from behind. Eew. She drew it out like *ooh-hoo-hoo-hoo*. She shuddered again, laughing.

Where was he touching you? On your shoulders?

Yeah. And he should know better, being the police.

Yeah well at least he'd be good for cheap pot.

What? Oh yeah.

There was a skinny guy in some of the photos, with a missing front tooth, scraggly black hair, and tinted sunglasses.

JESSE SAID, SO I'M HEADIN' OVER TOMORROW, IF YOU GUYS WANT A RIDE.

Oh yeah, where to, Van?

No, but I can drop you off. Gonna go up to the Interior.

Yeah, you guys going camping?

No, she's going to that blockade. Ray took a sip of beer and put the bottle down, sucking his teeth.

Oh, no way! That's so exciting! Jimmy and Lucy were excited.

Well, I don't know, you know, I just want to check it out. But Ray doesn't think it's such a good idea.

I didn't say that.

Yes you did, but I don't wanna argue. I just want to see for myself.

Aw, do whatever you want. I just think, you know, with the kid, you're just not just on your own anymore.

Are you going to take Sarah with you? Lucy was trying to divert the conversation, get back to the main topic.

Yeah. Well I'm not going to count on you to protect me, that's not why I love you.

I didn't say that. Why d'you take what I say?

You said – well, hey, why don't you come too?

Not interested.

See? Why not, check it out.

Look, it's just a bunch of idiots. I know those guys.

No, you can't just say –

Aw just. He waved his hand and took another drink.

OK, OK. Sorry, guys. Jesse gave them a smile.

Hey, no problem. You gotta work these things out, you know.

Long as you're talkin'. That's what I always say, hey? Long as you're talkin'.

TOM CAME OUT AT AROUND EIGHT, DRINKING A CUP OF COFFEE, NO SHIRT ON. His chest was hairless and his nipples were small brown dots on his chest. He looked in the car and then went back in.

He came out a few minutes later, still just wearing track pants, carrying some masking tape. He took some flowers out of a box and put them on the car, and a doll on the front of the hood. People kept pulling up on the street, three got into the driveway, the rest parked in the ditch. Jeff walked out wearing his suit pants and a shirt and tie.

Hey, so that's starting to look pretty good.

Yeah, it's not so bad, eh?

But we gotta get it done, eh? Getting the ball an' chain on, may as well do it up right.

Soon, the street was full of cars and trucks pulling in and out. A minivan pulled up, honking, and ushers and bridesmaids got out, the guys with fresh haircuts, in their suit vests, younger brothers, and the girls in longer versions of the dresses the little ten-year-olds were wearing.

Later, the car with the doll on its hood pulled up again. Guys stood around smoking, flicking ash into the flowerbeds.

Mary and her mother came out of the house carrying wrapped stuff in cardboard boxes. Mary perched one on the bumper and her mother opened the trunk. Mary looked at her watch. It was twenty after eleven. Her dad was lining people up on the lawn, pointing his camera like a dog's wet nose.

JENNIFER ON A COMMON TOPIC: HEY, YOU KNOW THOSE ROLLING PAPERS YOU GAVE US?

What?

Oh, you know the ones with the maple leaf flag on 'em?

Oh yeah, weren't they funny? Now Lucy and Jimmy remembered.

Oh yeah, my kid's like, hey what are these?

Oh no, gotta hide, eh? Hide from our parents, hide from our kids. One of Lucy's theories.

Oh no, usually I don't, I mean, I don't get fucked up when they're around but that's the same.

Oh yeah.

Yeah, usually, if it's just like regular he just ignores them, right? But these were so colourful and they were doing like flags at school or whatever.

OK, CHAIRS FOR EVERYONE. Mary carried them onto the concrete apron around the pool.

Up, good pool here though, Tom. Ray was still in the water. Have to do the FOD patrol.

Jesse had some more wine. Oh what's that. One of your military terms?

Yeah, you know, lookin' for garbage. Foreign object debris.
Just relax, grow your hair a bit buddy.

Oh, I know. I know I've been hiking around the past few weeks trying to burn off this fat I had in the Forces. You know, all that fucking greasy food they give you, and all you're doing all the time is sitting around. Man, it just builds on you.

Yep, getting lazy. Have to go to the gym next. Well, not tomorrow. Tomorrow I think I'll put my back out moving, have to call in sick.

Yeah sure, why not.

Hey, so like Finning's looking for mechanics.

Oh really?

Yeah, so like you should drop by there. Yeah, they're always looking.

Good company to work for.

Yeah. Now that I've learned how to slack off. In the Forces. Got my *if you've got time to clean you've got time to lean* education. Edjumacation.

Yeah, no kidding eh? I don't know man, I, man I know you were in it, you know, the military and all, and so you gotta defend it, but when I just figured, you know, there's more submarines at the West Edmonton Mall eh? I mean, our navy doesn't even –

Yeah, you know, well, that's what they've got. I don't care anymore.

H<small>EY</small>, <small>SO LIKE DID WE TELL YOU ABOUT THAT PARTY OUR FRIEND</small> T<small>REVOR HAD</small>?
Yeah so he went and got all this stuff from Crappy Tire, right? Yeah
so he went and got all this stuff from Crappy Tire right, volleyball
net, chairs, croquet, and we were just like wrecking the shit out of it.

Oh yeah, we're, we were just whaling on the stuff. Broke mallets,
and we were playin' some wicked stuff, everyone's totally wrecked, at
midnight playin' croquet and trippin' –

Yeah I bet you were trippin', that acid pot you're smoking, man this
B.C. bud's freakin' toxic –

– yeah tripping on the hoops. And the neighbours or whatever, they're
like calling his landlord, Trev's, cuz, and the police, and the landlord
calls 'im and says don't worry about it. And the next day –

Yeah, yeah, the next day they just brought the stuff, on the Monday,
back to Canadian Tire and said this is *shit*, what kinda Chinese crap
you guys sellin', we want our money back. And no questions asked.
So now we call it the Canadian Tire Party Rental.

But like Trev, he was out of control. He moved in that place after his
divorce, and so like people are saying hey let's get some rock and roll
going, and he's like no. Just country. Just wants to sit there feeling
sorry for himself, you know? But don't get me wrong, people still
came by in waves, though. We just slept there, had the kid and just
crashed. Didn't want to drive after all that.

HE HELPED CARRY THE CHAIRS OUT TO THE TRUCK. OK, and his father opened the back. Alright, we got that squared away. He brushed his hands together.

So, what else you guys up to?

Oh well, you know, your mother and I are planning on maybe checking out the west coast of the Island. We haven't done that much, so we'll just toodle around. See what's there.

Yeah, I guess you're all set now.

Well, that's the thing.

HE WAS A CANADIAN, AND TALKED LIKE A THRIFTY TELEGRAM, A BRIEF EMAIL, TXT.

SAID *FUCK YOU* TOO MANY TIMES TO TOO MANY PEOPLE.

Hey guys did I tell you about her little friend? There's this, he's just the cutest little kid, right? He's really cute and he comes over and says Can Sarah come out and play? So it's good, she's making friends.

Oh, she's great Jess.

Yeah, she's active, cuz she's around lots of different adults, and independent.

Oh, I got you guys a present. Here. She passed over a painted rock the size of her fist. Jimmy turned the rock over, it said Jesus Loves You. On top was painted a Native girl's face.

Oh, that's great. Let me see that. He passed it to her. Oh hilarious. Yeah, we've gotta put it in the garden, put it somewhere good.

Yeah, so like we were there and she's like just got freaked out by the Happy Rock Lady. You know, she just saw everywhere there's these happy rocks. But Dave was all stressed about it! Yes! It's cuz of how he's a really heavy atheist, and he only told Ben about God a little while ago. Cuz there was this kid eh? And he was like God made this or God did that or God said it's OK, or whatever. Like God was this regular person. So he had to tell him about it, and Wendy's OK, it's just Dave. We were over there and I just felt like leaving, you know? I mean, he's my brother and everything, but he was being rude, just plain rude. You know, I just felt like leaving. And everyone couldn't believe it. Wendy was just like, looking at him. I don't know, I mean I know he had things on his mind, I could tell, but he didn't, you know, specifically tell me. And he didn't have to be so uptight about it. But did he tell you? He was up for the lead role in the play they're putting on, that's why he was so stressed.

So did he get it?

Oh yeah, excellent, eh?

Oh, we have to go see it.

Yeah, you should.

Yeah, we will.

So what do you wanna do now? You guys want to do something? Go to the beach, the lake?

What lake, no, I don't know.

Oh I don't know, that sounds good. Nice to get out, catch some rays.

OK I'm going to phone the parks see if it's open. Ray sprang to action, grabbed the cordless.

What?

The lake. They closed it for algae.

So you know Pam's in town, hey?

Huh? Who? Not –

Yeah, so like Pamela Lee Anderson –

Pamela Anderson *Lee*.

Oh really?

Really.

Yeah, I guess that makes sense eh? Cuz she – anyway, guess her mother's getting some award from the Valley First Nations group, they're, they're honouring her.

They're honouring Pamela? For what, having teepees on her chest?

No, her mom. Her mom is Native. You didn't know that?

Oh no, really.

Yeah, no yeah, it's true. So.

So –

So yeah so she's in town, think she might be down there. Cuz you know, Dave went to high school with her.

Oh really, excellent.

Yeah, I think they actually had a date or two, back before she became popular.

HE PULLED THE TAMPON OUT OF HER AND PUT IT NEXT TO THE BED. He started licking her and she rolled over, sat on him, closing her eyes.

I DON'T KNOW, I WANT A FENCE THERE THOUGH. I just don't want them, they just look right over, like that guy, who's that guy, on that show –

Yeah, I know –

How about a hedge? Looks nicer. Lucy was pushing the hedge quotient.

Yeah, but too much work. Jeff thought of those things.

They're not cheap either, Mary said.

Nice cedar hedge?

We haven't had a lot of luck with cedar, either.

Oh, but a hedge would be so pretty.

He walked behind her.

Yeah, but the thing was it was his boat. Kevin, Costner's, Kevin Costner's right? And it was her job to take care of the kids, teach them the rules, because it was his boat so that's why he had to leave at the end. Cuz you have to, well, you know, you know what I'm talking about.

He was on a boat?

Oh yeah, we're on the same wavelength. Yeah it was excellent, it opened up and everything.

What, the boat? She had her head down, her jacket slipping around her bare shoulders. Silver mules on, and she held the cigarette pointing up away from the ringlets falling around her face. They walked past a white car with paper flowers on it and a doll in a white dress as a hood ornament. Other cars for the wedding were in the street, Shriners' little cars after a parade. Streaks in a car's finish, dried dust on its windshield, showed up in the bright sunlight.

A guy in his forties with white sidewalls came running out of a house, followed by kids. He opened up a car and ran back into the house, he was in stocking feet and a three-piece suit.

They turned to walk down an alley. A guy stood by his car, they heard his voice before they saw him. He was drinking a glass mug of coffee, with milk. They could hear a car honking behind them, she looked back and saw a kid in the back seat of the car lean over the tilted passenger seat, pressing the horn. She was dressed for church.

The guy drinking milky coffee was talking to a woman holding a cup of black coffee. He had on a casual shirt and pants, and slippers. The hood of the car was up.

I don't see what they need me for, he was saying. They're so disorganized.

Oh, I know, the woman said, holding her coffee cup with both hands.

He kept talking as they walked past a woman leaning into her hatchback. She wore beige shorts and a white top. When she straightened up she spat in the grass and closed the hatchback.

And they had these amazing effects. At the end, they're on the jet skis and they all hit each other and there's this amazing explosion.

So it's just bad driving, eh? We could go out with your brother any time for that. Go out on the fucking water. Lose your fucking shirt, money you don't have, paying for gas but –

Hey what're you *talking* about?

Well, I just can't believe he did that. He's like so stupid to bet everything on a boat, and. But. Sounds totally like *Mad Max*.

Totally.

Mad Max on the Water eh?

Fuckin' rights.

So what's she going to do now? They're in hock –

Aw c'mon, they'll work it out.

There's nothing to work out. Owing a lot of money? All you can do is owe it or pay it.

Yeah, I think they're gonna talk to the East Indian.

Oh yeah, that'll do it. That'll be a wise move.

THE MUSIC SOUNDED LIKE R.E.M. OR CHRIS DE BURGH, JIMMY COULDN'T TELL. Someone was knocking at the door and Mary told him, Don't open it yet. Who the fuck is it? They laughed while she scraped the pot into her hand. He went and opened the door, just as Jesse said from outside, Hey, open up in there, it's me.

Hey, so how's it going? Just wanted to see you guys before you head back.

Oh good, yeah, nice to see you again. Lucy hugged Jesse and Sarah. So how's it going?

Oh pretty good. Drag about yesterday.

Yeah, well, we waited around, what can you do? We had a good time. *I* had a good time anyways.

Yeah so, oh, you were rolling a joint, eh? Good idea, I could use one. Hey there kiddo, you better eat up, it's breakfast. She opened the baby bag and gave Sarah part of a McMuffin. Yeah, so what'd you think of Raymond? I call him Raymond.

Oh, he's pretty nice.

Yeah, well, we'll just see. I don't know, I have to really focus now, going back to school, eh? That's part of why I moved up here and I don't want to get crazy for some guy who's just going to distract me. She laughed, her laugh was husky, real. She blinked her eyes, shook her hair, then stared straight ahead.

You'll figure it out.

Oh yeah, I always do. But Jeff, that guy, he was crazy. When I finally told him *Enough!* he was like, crying, and he wanted to come around.

And he'd stand outside my window. I was getting pissed off. But did I tell you what he did?

No, don't think so. They passed around the joint.

Mmm, thanks. He was doing this job right? This contract for some house or whatever, and he was supposed to buy all this carpet or whatever, and he had like three thousand dollars and he just fucked off with it.

Oh no! Wow, that's fucked up.

Yeah, he went to the store at the end of the day, or he was supposed to anyways, and he just grabbed the next ferry over to Van. Yeah, so he's probably –

Oh man, cuz he's just fucked himself for working there, eh?

Oh yeah, probably for all over. You know, it's good for at least a province-wide warrant. So he just took off. Vamoosed. Skedaddled. But I don't know.

Cuz you get tempted, right?

Huh, what's that?

You get, I don't know, you just get tempted. Why not? Like once –

Oh sure, maybe –

Once when I was working for, at that bar, what was it, at the university?

Yeah, ummm –

Felena's, and on Thursday nights, you know, it was mega busy –
All the White Russians –

And Brown Cows –

Paralyzers, Creamsicles, Sangrias –

B-52s, special coffees, Harvey Wallbangers –

Sex with a Virgin –

Sex on the Beach, A Long Slow Screw Up Against the Wall –

Abortions –

Shooter girls.

Yeah, it was fuckin' crazy, and so we'd sometimes, we'd like gross like
twenty grand and this was back in the eighties when that meant something, twenty grand from two or three bars, and special functions
being on and I'd have to put it all in the safe and I'd just think, what
time is the next person coming in? It'd be one or two in the morning,
and there'd be no one in till eleven or noon, and I could get the first
ferry, just take off.

Oh sure ten grand, twenty grand, at least five grand minimum, but
not, not like –

No, not for three grand, but you know, it's like that old joke, guys say
to this woman would you sleep with me for a billion dollars and she
says, well, I have to admit I would, and he says would you sleep with
me for fifteen dollars and she's like what do you think I am, a ho, and
he's like, well, that's been established baby, now we're just haggling.

OH YEAH, I GET WHAT YOU'RE SAYING, I SEE WHERE YOU'RE GOING WITH THIS.

And your point is? Lucy mock-frowned, headed back into the kitchen. Over her shoulder: Jess you don't feel guilty, do you?

No. Yes. I mean, I don't know how I pick them.

Yeah, maybe go for guys who are slightly less obsessive.

He was a good fuck though eh, I'll give 'im that. Man, I don't think I'm that superficial you know? I mean, now, I don't just want some guy with a great body. I mean, he has to have one, she laughed.

Yeah, but that can't be your only consideration.

Yeah, not any more. I've gone through too many guys, though. Ed was right, he said I was a slut. No I wasn't, I mean, I hardly screwed around. You know, not much. But a lot of guys.

Well, whatever you want, Jess, I mean, just do what you want as long as you're happy with yourself and you're not hurting other people. You know.

Yeah, at least you changed your underwear.

Oh, you guys! Changed my underwear, of course I changed my underwear.

Oh, are you sure you didn't forget?

Huh, oh gross, get out. You guys.

JIMMY CARRIED OUT THE POT OF MUSHROOM TEA. Hey this is hot.

Don't spill any! Valuable liquid. I don't think the carpet's going to appreciate it any.

Yeah, no kidding, eh?

Oh sure, just set 'er down. That's the way.

So you guys want to spark one up while we let it sit there?

Yeah, sure.

Oh not me, no I'll get too tired. So did you manage to get some Sid? He wanted Sid.

But of *course* – in a fake French accent. Yeah that friend of ours, Randy, he had a lot.

So you think you could get some?

Oh, from us, or from Randy?

I don't know. Whatever. Would he be around now?

Oh, umm, no, I think he went to Van for the weekend. But how much d'you want?

I don't know, maybe six hits.

Yeah cuz we've got about twenty-five.

What? Really?

Oh yeah, well, some are cubes and some are tabs. So some of the cubes're doubles, or one-and-a-halfs and stuff.

Whoa, no way, really?

What, does he make it himself?

No, but this friend of his. I went over today to get it.

What, to his friend's?

No, to Randy's.

THEY WENT OVER TO JESSE AND HAYLEY'S PLACE.

Jimmy and Lucy climbed into the back of Jeff's car. It was an old Cadillac, the red velvet and chrome trimmings like a turkey in a tuxedo.

What, oh, no holy shit bars.

No way, class all the way. Don't worry. You won't feel the road.

Good, cuz I barf.

OK, well, we'll just make sure – he pushed a button up front and her window rolled down – you try and miss the side of the car eh?

Oh Jesus, yeah. Don't worry about it. Oh that wine. Killer.

Yeah, should'na switched.

Yeah, should stick with bottles. Not boxes.

At least screw caps.

THEY PASSED HIS DAD GOING THE OTHER WAY ON THEIR WAY OVER TO JESSE'S. They laughed at each other. At Jesse's they knocked and she let them in laughing.

Dave was just here, eh? Yeah, with Grandma.

Yeah, we saw them. Dad I mean, we saw Dad. Was everyone here?

No, didn't see Dad.

So, quite the place, have to say.

The phone rang and she picked it up. Huh? No, yeah, they just got here. OK. Yeah, sure, why wouldn't she? Oh yeah, it'll be great. OK, when you leave. She hung up.

Yeah not bad, eh? I was lucky, getting on the waiting list and then I got one almost right away. But it's stupid, you know why? Cuz it's cheaper rent but my welfare's lower now. So why should I?

Yeah, that's fucked. They all sat around the cluttered living room. It was comfortable. There were posters, framed, on the walls and a stereo by the TV.

I know, it's totally fucked. The phone rang and she picked it up. Hey how are ya? Oh yeah. So you don't wanna come over? How come? Well – no, but that's silly. Yeah, sure. Bye. That was Jessica. She doesn't wanna come now. So you guys want a beer?

I wouldn't say no.

Yeah, sure.

Jimmy went to the fridge and pulled out a couple ciders and a Genuine Draft.

You guys want ciders?

Yep, you betcha.

So Jess, said Ray, you know what you're going to be up to this week?

Nope. Not right now. Ask me tomorrow.

Cuz I got my friend coming in and I'm gonna show 'im around and I figured we could get together.

Yeah, that'll be good.

Yeah, so like, you know Pete. He was going with Melissa.

Yeah, I know Melissa. Nice girl. Got that biker chick look all the guys go for, apparently. The phone rang and she picked it up.

Ray sat down next to Jimmy on the sofa. Hey, did you see that thing on the coast on TV last night?

No, can't say I did. Jimmy leaned back and sipped some beer.

Yeah, they were like talking about they were doing this book, but it was all this old stuff, so it sounded like *Leave It to Beaver*, you know?

Jesse hung up the phone again. So what about Melissa and Pete?

Had to get a restraining order on him, Ray says. Beatin' on 'er. If there's one thing I can't stand it's guys beatin' on women. So did I tell you Jess I went over there, you know, I never, I never knew Pete right? And I get there and I go up to the door and I ring the bell and this guy answers the door and I go, Are you Pete and he's like, No, are you? That was Mike, another friend of Melissa's and he was waiting for Pete just like me. So eventually . . . everyone just wanted to pound him one. Yeah, the only problem is Pete used to be everyone's connection. Never met the guy but always got pot from him. OK I'm gonna go.

OK Jess, I'll see ya later – give you a call tomorrow, eh? I'm headin' out.

Yep. See ya. So like I couldn't believe Dave. He doesn't even take his shoes off. He's like, no, I can wait down here. Even Grandma kinda looked at him kinda funny. You know, I'm showing her around.

He can't relax, that's his problem, Lucy said. I know.

The phone rang and Jesse picked it up. Hi. OK. You sure you don't want to come? OK, fine, don't worry about it. Look no one's going to worry. I mean, you know. You know, no one'd think that.

LIKE.

YOU KNOW.

BECAUSE WHEN YOU LOOK AT ALL THE FACTORS, YOU KNOW ALL YOU'VE GOT TO DO IS TO GET EVERYONE AT THE SAME TABLE TALKING. And you know, then you can work things out, as long as everyone agrees on a few basic principles. But they're not interested, you know certain people, in this. And so they're like, they'd rather be out there protesting and you know, not working towards something constructive.

AND SO IN THE END, YOU JUST HAVE TO SAY, YOU KNOW WHAT'S THE POINT.

Jesse says, Yeah, so like it's her acne, she had an outbreak of it, so she doesn't wear a swimsuit.

Oh, is she the key pin to all this, the kingpin?

Yeah she's kind of my water-skiing. No, it's just that Jason phoned and asked if she was going to be there. He's amazing, wait till you see him, Lucy. Sorry, Jimmy. No offense.

Oh, real hot stuff, is he?

No, he's nice. Yeah, and his friend's a goalie for the Kings.

So, d'you want to smoke one?

Yeah, you guys got some stuff from Tom?

Yep, came over yesterday. Major production, though.

Yeah, he's kind of paranoid. Sometimes he doesn't have it.

Yeah, I wasn't too much into forking over ninety bucks and he like takes off. He kind of slurred his words. I mean I know you know him and Wendy and Dave.

Yeah, well I just know him through Wendy, eh? I mean I knew him in high school. He was like, in a major accident. Didn't you notice anything weird about him?

He was a bit, I don't know, not really.

No, cuz he was in this accident, and he had a steering wheel, into his chest. So he had this major surgery.

I'VE BEEN READING THESE BOOKS, ABOUT HEDGES. Jimmy and Lucy were walking around one night.

So . . . ?

Well, it's a very exhaustive field. There's all kinds of shit out there.

I'm sure there is. Do they talk about hedge-throwing? She gave him a bit of a push.

Oh yeah, exactly, how'd you guess?

No! Lucy laughed again.

Yes! No really, there's a report by a police commission or something about kids from the East End wandering around throwing little kids into hedges.

Hilarious. Paranoid, eh?

Oh yeah, exactly. And it has all the details of how it happens, and the Hedge-Throwers gang structure. Like, have you ever heard of Ladner Leprechauns?

No, what is it, a gift shop? She narrowed her eyes and puckered her lips at him.

THEY WALKED INTO THE HOUSE. Oh this is so good. You guys have it so good. You've really done it nice.

Yeah, you think so?

Oh yeah you've got to, you know, do your own space. That's what it's all about. Hey Jeff, don't you like that? We should do that.

Sure. Whatever. We can do whatever we want, it'll be our house.

Oh yeah, isn't that so great. I can't believe it. She scrunched up her nose as she smiled. It was attractive. Oh, have you guys been following the – she flicked a finger at the newspaper – trial?

Yeah.

No. Oh, he has. Major event.

Yeah, so much of it is so stupid. It was OK I guess, as a trial.

Yeah. Restrained.

Yeah but can you believe that she'd – that they'd –

Oh I know. But yeah, people who are really depraved, forever.

HEY HAVE YOU GUYS SEEN THIS? They were in Jesse's room, smoking a joint. No, wait, first of all, this is for you. She handed them a bag of mushrooms.

Oh great, thanks a lot Jess.

Hey, no problem. But check this out. She reached up onto her dresser, and pulled down some earrings.

Oh right on, they're –

They're little dream catchers. I got a set, with a necklace. I know the girl who does them, eh?

Oh yeah, these are great. She giggled. They're cute.

They agreed: they were the greatest.

THEY WENT TO THE BEACH AFTER ALL. Some people were going to be there, Pam, and the goalie's friend, and they could go water skiing. They got lost going up the mountain to the lake. They took a wrong left turn and ended lost in the warm mountain air.

But they found the lake and parked on the stone beach. Jesse knew some people there, a guy had a cell phone. Sarah wandered to the water and sat down.

Oh, guess I'll have to change her now. She was talking to a big guy in golf shirt and shorts, blond curls.

They dicked around a while, watched the para-skiing operation. It was forty-five bucks and you were only in the air for like five minutes tops.

SO WHAT DO YOU THINK OF WHAT YOUR FATHER'S DONE? They were at his grandmother's place, a condo in Coquitlam.

Hmm, oh, do you mean with the boat? I dunno. His, he can do whatever he wants.

I just think it's marvellous. You know, he's very clever. He always was.

YEAH, SO YOU HEARD ABOUT JIMMY'S LITTLE INCIDENT?

What, no?

Yeah he – it was hilarious. It was late at night and he's home and he gets up to take out the garbage and he goes outside and hears this noise.

No.

Yeah, coming from the garage.

What was it?

Well, that's what I'm coming to if you'll just give me a chance. Oh, and so he's like he's got whatever, the stuff for the – and he's down there, and he hears it, right, and it's like, you know, heavy breathing coming from the garage right, like huffing.

I REMEMBER WHEN I USED TO GO WITH HIM TO HIS LITTLE HOCKEY BANQUETS.

Who?

That guy, Ken. He's the guy who plays for the Kings. Yeah, I guess he's just up here. Off-season.

Sure, like Don Greschner's kid, played for the Rangers in the seventies, he owned a car dealership in Cold Lake.

JIMMY WAS OBSESSING. No, but the worst thing is that it starts being this big example in your life, he said. Like instead of, like if you're – and you get these blinkers in your eyes, right? Mental ones, you can't think of anything else, right, you're afraid even to talk sometimes.

Yeah, no, when you're working, you know. Lucy was soothing and realistic.

Yeah, so like, I go to rinse out a yogurt container, and I didn't rinse out this pan and it's like – urk – guilt! Plea bargain!

Yeah yeah, and all of the sudden you're like, oops, I like doing that. She thought of fisting him.

Yeah, it's the way things get rolled out, you know? Like all of the sudden we're like better than the Americans.

So what movie'd you get?

Centerfold Girls. It's supposed to be great.

I DON'T KNOW, I JUST THINK THEY'RE PRETTY AMAZING. Karma coma music playing, J'maic'n aroma. Jimmy and Lucy walking around, again.

Oh look, there's a good alley for you. Three Vancouver Specials in a row.

Aren't they beautiful.

I don't know, maybe. They're something.

Nice hedges.

True.

OH YOU FEEL SO GOOD INSIDE ME.

Well I was certainly enjoying it. I always get –

Yeah, I could barely take it. What, were you storing it up.

Well, you know, it's been a couple days. You should cut your nails.

Oh, and look who's talking! You have to be careful with my little pussy. It's delicate. I'm made of petals.

Oh, sorry, got a bit excited. I like feeling your stubble on my face.

Hey, I had a bath.

Yeah, I love it. I love how it feels inside you. You're so tight. Even like –

Of course. I want to be.

Yeah, even like after you came and we rolled over. I mean d'you like it when after you come, I keep, you know?

Oh yeah. Lots of excitement going on.

Yeah but god, when –

He shuddered a bit.

SO HOW'S THE OLD FUCK MACHINE DOIN'? Ready for more action?

Anytime, babe.

You wish.

A guy walked by their window. Black hair in a crew cut, black baggy pants.

Yeah, I could just eat you all day long. I love it when you get all excited.

He lay on his front against her, playing with her belly button ring. She pushed his hand away. After a minute he turned over and stuck his arm under his pillow. His shoulder pulled back. He turned away from her. He heard a car alarm pop outside. A car started. He rolled over onto his back again. She moved back against him, her face on his chest. He slid his hand down her back, feeling the cilia at the top of her ass.

Small hair, the fuzzy hair stuff.

They drifted off to sleep.

OH YEAH, THEY WERE SURE I'D WON THE LOTTERY, RAY SAID. My mom was like, phoning everyone.

Oh, I know and you're like. Jimmy leaned against the fridge.

Yeah, I mean, I was Mom, it's not that much.

YEAH, WE COULD SPLIT THE RENT, SPLIT THE PHONE. Why not? You've got your kid, I have mine. Yeah, you like this song? Yeah, I got this tape from a friend of mine, she's crazy. You know, and we could like baby sit for each other. Course, that means we couldn't party together. You know, whatever. I'd like to, you know, get some hours, get some work. And with the kid. You know, I can't do everything.

Why don't you sit over here?

EVERYTHING BECAME A MAJOR ACT. Washing his face, it was like the water he was wiping away was a victim and he was as horrible as the murderers by letting the water fall into the sink.

BEN WALKED AROUND THE ROOM AS THE ADULTS TALKED, THEIR CONVERSATION A LIGHT HUM BEHIND THE CLICKING NOISE HIS WOODEN SPOON MADE. He hit everything, the noise was a science fiction movie.

So how're you doing?

Oh, you know.

Yeah.

Just, you know.

Yeah, it's OK.

Yeah, good.

JUST THIS STUPID JOB THING.

Yeah, I know. Don't worry.

YEAH, SO LIKE I TOLD YOU ABOUT JEFF, EH? That guy I was seein'? He was like, you know, sometimes he'd get really gross. I mean like, you know one time we were talking about Van, and he was just freaking on the West End, you know, he was like, oh it's like horrible there, and you know why he's saying that? The gays. He's like, you know, his friend Jason was over and he was like, oh I can't stand the fucking West End. And I'm like why? Cuz I know, but I just want him to say it, to acknowledge it. I can't stand it when people are ignorant like that. You know, it's just ignorant. And I said to him, I said well you know people could just say that about me, and how would you feel about that. And he's just like, he's all flustered, eh? Doesn't know what to say. And that's when he freaked. The radio was on, and it was like some L7 or something, you know, and he's like what is this shit. Turn that fucking crap off. Why do we have to listen to that? And you know, it was really –

I DON'T KNOW, I WAS JUST. I don't know I was just pissed off. You know? Cuz it was my place. And he's just like freaking.

So, I think I'm going to get a stereo. Yup. Need the upgrade. Jimmy and Jeff were on the patio.

Yeah, good idea.

Yeah, well, I figured that.

Yeah.

Yeah, well.

Huh.

You know, tunes.

Oh yeah, sure. Necessity.

Mary came out, ta da.

Hey those look great.

Yeah, excellento, babe.

They got set up with nachos and fixings, the snack food of a summer's day.

Oh yeah tunes are a necessity of life.

Serious.

But, you know what you should do. He had some nachos.

No, what do you mean?

You should get one through the *Buy and Sell*.

Yeah, that's what I was thinking. Good idea.

Yeah, sure, you can get a good deal.

Yeah I don't need anything perfect.

No, you just want to, you just need some tunes.

Yeah.

I mean, you just have to listen to it. Yeah, I'll get it. We have one, cuz we were selling that stuff.

Right the –

Back in a sec.

Those.

He came back out with the paper.

OK here it is.

Alright, what section . . . OK. . . .

Figure it out there. There's an index.

Here we are. . . .

They usually have quite a lot.

Oh yeah, there's some deals.

Oh, sure.

Yeah, not bad.

I'm gonna get a beer, you?

Uh, yeah.

Gotcha.

Hey look, here's one.

Jeff called from inside. What's that?

Getting married. Selling his stereo cuz he's getting married.

Loser.

Yeah, no kidding. Up, life is over. May as well be miserable.

Yeah, all you gotta do is make sure it's not hot. You know.

Yeah.

I don't know about you, but I don't want to buy – you know, ask for the book or something.

Oh yeah, no, I'd –

Cuz I was looking at this boat, and, you know, I asked why the number'd been scraped off.

Oh yeah, no way.

Yeah, sure. You know, he was saying he'd had it, it was his boat. So why's the number scraped off?

Yeah.

And repainted. Yeah, they couldn't answer that. So, I don't know, you know, I figured, so I don't want my boat stolen, I'm not going to buy a stolen one.

Makes sense.

HE TURNED IT UP.

Hey, what's this?

Just some tunes. Some rock.

I think I'd prefer something else.

I'm gonna.

Yep, get used to it. They get to change the music. No doubt. Don't have a hope.

THEY SET UP A CROQUET GAME, JUST THE TWO OF THEM PLAYING. The hoops were scattered in the tall grass, you could barely see them in the Ladner twilight.

PEOPLE STOOD AROUND THE YARD DRINKING AS THEY PLAYED THROUGH.

AFTER A WHILE IT GOT DARK AND THEY STOPPED.

SHE BIT HARD ON HIS NIPPLE, TWISTING IT AROUND. Her pubic mound was on his stomach. He moved around a bit, his hands on her hips.

I'M GOING TO HAVE A SHOWER, YOU WANT ONE?

No. Oh, jeez. God knows I should after. She stood on one foot pulling on her panties, her knee in the air.

OK.

Yeah, oh, here comes some more.

YEAH . . . WELL.

Yeah, well what?

Sarah made a bee-line for the Mr. Turtle pool. Her cousin started splashing before she got to it. Water sprayed up from the hose hooked up to the pool.

Jesse dragged the baby bag over to next to the table and dropped it. She dug out a pack of smokes and sat down.

Hey, so I got my lip done. Jesse leaned forward, sticking out her bottom lip. The big white table glared in the sun. Brightly coloured toys and playground equipment all around the yard, cedar tree fringes beyond the fence like prison guard towers.

No way! Lucy leaned forward, smiling. Let's see.

See?

Yeah, not bad.

Hey can you see it?

Yep, said Jimmy. Where'd you get it done? Sarah moved out of the pool and walked over to the swing. Little Ben sat down in the pool.

Oh there's that girl in town, downtown, you know her? She opened up that place on River, it's near the bakery. It's really *ster*-ile.

Oh yeah, they all are now.

Yeah, you have to be. No, she like went through everything, you know, showed how they do the needles, it was like, remember when I got my tattoo?

Oh yeah, same thing.

Same rigmarole. Yeah, you know, that time I can still remember it, there's this big guy, this big disgusting guy with hairy arms like spilling over his latex gloves. But he was clean, though. So did I tell you?

No, what?

Oh, you know about Jason.

So you want to smoke a jay? Jimmy pulled his stash out.

Huh, oh yeah, sure, of course. Well, cuz you know, I knew him a long time ago. Jason.

Oh yeah.

Yeah and he calls me up last week, eh? And he's like, oh Jess, I haven't seen you in a long time, why don't we get together. And I'm like sure, you know, whatever. And, I don't know, maybe I didn't sound like I was jumping up and down for joy or nothin' and he was like, what's the matter, don't you want to see me?

Insecure motherfucker. Oh well, I'm sorry I didn't, you know, like open my legs. Mary lit the joint in Jimmy's fingers.

Oh yeah, exactly, a real baby. But, I don't know, he can be pretty nice.

Yeah, Jimmy said. I saw him that time we were over, right? And he was, he was alright.

Oh sure, yeah, instant asshole, just add beer.

Oh really, drag.

Yeah, but you know, I'll see.

YEAH, BUT IT CAN BE, YOU REMEMBER THAT TIME I HAD MY NOSE PIERCED? Everyone was like –

Jesse was reminiscing about the eighties.

Oh yeah, family calamity.

Yeah! Cuz they were like – I mean Mom's like, well, it's your nose, that's alright, but Grandma?

Oh yeah, what, did she freak out? Lucy didn't remember all of the nose-piercing incident.

Yeah she's like, you're in a gang, aren't you?

What?

Oh serious, for sure, she's like, you know, anything, they see it on TV and it's like, you're in a gang.

Kids on drugs.

Yeah, if only. No. She was thoughtful. No, but we had it pretty good. No but, you know, she can just like, I don't know, and she wants to take me to church.

What, your grandma? Jimmy butt in.

Yeah well, Catholic guilt, right?

Oh yeah.

Yeah, I mean I love her, she's my grandma right, but still. But she's harmless.

R, YOU KNOW. I mean, like mine were the worst.
akin' phone first thing in the morning. Yeah, one
hey're just totally fucking ragging me and I just
you, just fuck it all.

Oh yeah, she still loves you.

Oh, there's never any doubt about that. I mean, she can't really think I'm in a gang, though. Like what, I'm driving by people and shooting them?

Yeah, but on a skateboard. They always think it's skaters too.

Right. Oh yeah.

Ray took out a roach clip made from a rifle shell. They were in the kitchen. Yeah, so like, I should get you some mushrooms.

Oh, we've got a pretty good supply. We've got some now, got them from a friend of ours from Hornby. They're amazing.

Oh yeah. Yeah, well, I've got this friend, he's growing a big patch, no, he's got a couple different lots, eh?

You mean pot.

Yeah.

Cuz you know my connection, it was a friend of ours, he left town for Calgary.

Oh, so you need to get set up.

Well, we're doing OK, but haven't really –

Yeah, this guy has pretty good prices. They're not great.

Yeah we were paying what, thirty-five to forty-five, but it was excellent hydro.

Like acid, eh?

Oh totally, great stones. And I didn't get too tired, which I hate.

Oh yeah, right. But this guy, one time he was going out to, you know, check. Hey Mary, you want to get going?

Yeah sure, where you wanna go?

I don't kno
there too an

Oh no. Trage

Yeah, gone. An
down, they were

Fuck. So a farmer.

Cops.

Oh yeah.

Farmer woulda just trim
cuz he has other fields, b
coulda made, I don't kno

Oh they're just kille
You know, on the fr
time I'm there and t
felt like saying fuck

So you want one?

Huh? No, those things'll burn a hole in your lungs.

Yeah, I'll have one.

Lucy passed the pack over.

Oh jeez, Mary goes. I haven't had one of these since that day we were over in Kits.

They're really sweet, eh? They lit up off her Zippo.

I think they coat the paper, Jeff said.

Yeah, so like that first puff you have this sweetness to cover up the stink.

Yeah, right.

So what's the plan?

Oh, didn't I tell you?

No, did you hear about something? Jimmy and Jennifer's mysterious boyfriend were in the kitchen.

Jimmy put the kettle on. How much should I put in here?

Oh, dump the whole batch. There's four of us, so, you know, don't want to be –

Yeah, guess so. He dumped the mushrooms into the pot.

Yeah, I'm going to get a power-washer.

Oh yeah, that sounds pretty good. Gonna buy one? Can you get them pretty cheap?

Gonna lease one. They're in the paper, and I can make it back in one Saturday.

Oh great.

Yeah, just set 'er up down by the dock there, at the marina. Work outside, catching the rays, you're laughin'.

Excellent.

Yeah and all the girls are like.

Oh yeah. The kettle came to a boil.

Yeah, OK, so just, yeah, that's great.

The kettle poured over the mushrooms.

JEFF WAS WEARING A PASTEL TANK TOP AND TRUNKS WHEN HE OPENED THE DOOR. Guys. Enter. I see you come bearing gifts.

Of course. Lucy had a six of cider under her arm. Point me to the fridge.

Oh yeah, I forgot, you've never been here before.

Yeah I woulda helped you on the move, but.

Oh yeah, sure, shift work.

THE SECTIONAL SOFA WAS ARRANGED AROUND A HUGE COFFEE TABLE. A couple of remotes lay on the table, bottles, chips. A cat was on Mary's lap.

YEAH, CUZ YOU KNOW, I WAS AT WORK. Jesse put the dream catcher earrings back on her dresser. The joint was dead.

Where, at the mounties?

No, not my new job. At the friendship centre. And people were talking about it there and they had a circle.

Hey, watch that run, eh?

Oh yeah, don't worry about this puppy. Jimmy held the joint.

Just goober it.

Under control.

D'you want the roach clip? It's over there. Jesse pointed at the wall unit.

Oh no, not him.

Yeah, no, I never use 'em. Strictly old school.

Not macho-mania here.

No, never used 'em.

Yeah, some people don't. Ray took the roach from Jimmy with his rifle shell.

Well, maybe if you cut your fingernails sometimes. Lucy shifted on the sofa, pulling on her cut-offs.

Now it isn't that, I just got used to, never needed it, Jimmy said.

Yeah? asked Ray.

Yeah, you only need a clip when you're passing it around, right?

Yeah, guess so.

Depends on if you have a filter or not.

Naw, doesn't matter.

Sometimes people just torch the end of it, burn it right down. Dave does.

No, I don't worry about that. Hotel. But I always smoked alone until I met Lucy.

Bachelor of the herb.

No, my girlfriends never smoked. I always smoked by myself.

Girlfriends –

Yeah well, whatever. Look who's –

Jesse and Ray looked at each other quickly.

Yeah, so I just got used to not using one.

SO WHO'S HIS GUY WHO'S COMING OVER? Jeff? Another Jeff?

Yeah, Jeff 2 we call him, Jennifer said.

And who're Jess and Ray?

Umm, they know Jimmy's girlfriend Lucy. And there's Jessica too.

Yeah, she works in this lawyer's office.

Lucy and Jimmy're getting married?

Nope. Just got engaged.

And she has a kid.

Who?

Lucy.

No, no, she doesn't. Not yet, anyway.

OK, so who's got the other kid?

What, at their place? Oh that's Jesse.

Right, and her daughter.

Sarah, yeah. Oh, she's really cute.

THEY WERE BOTH REALLY STONED. He lay on his back on the bed as she got undressed. She lay across the bed with her head on his stomach.

Jesus, where'd that come from? Didn't you have enough to drink?

Yeah well, you know, I'm not gonna – I can still perform.

Never known it to be otherwise. Or I didn't notice, anyway. Like I should talk.

I like it when you're drunk.

I know you do. What are you going to do about it.

Something. I like how your voice goes. I can always tell.

Oh, I like how your eyes go.

No, like when you've had a joint and I get home or whatever, and yeah, and your eyes, too. They're always sparkling.

Mmm, come here, mister sexy man.

And I like the way you always kiss me really – hey!

Now you just be quiet. She pushed him over onto his front. Or I'm going to have to spank you.

Really. Well, then.

So do you know what you're going to bring?

No, you?

Yeah I made a fruit pizza.

Hey, so long as it's not lawn pizza. Hee hee.

ALLISON AND ANDREA CAME OVER WITH JESSE AND HALEY. They sat around and smoked, watched a porn movie called *Ass Job*.

Reason to get a car, Andrea said. She wore a big sweater, and acid wash jeans tucked into cowboy boots. Allison kept nuzzling her crotch. They were totally in love.

So it's going to happen. Allison had a conspiratorial look. Like a pirate or a politician.

What? What, what? Lucy was excited, they all were.

We're going to go on *Donahue*.

I thought it was *Geraldo*.

No, no, it's *Donahue*.

Oh no, what for?

You guys? Both of you?

Why?

Yeah.

Her mom.

Yeah, as long as she doesn't talk it's OK.

She can't talk. We would just die.

OH MY GOD, ISN'T THAT AMAZING? I know, I just can't believe it.

YEAH AND SO HE GOES, WELL YOU MAY AS WELL START WHAT YOU, I MEAN, YOU KNOW, FINISH WHAT YOU START, AND I'M LIKE WHOA, YOU KNOW, I MEAN, IT'S LIKE AS IF YOU KNOW I'M TAKING A BRIBE TO GO DOWN IN THE FIFTH.

I know, like major paranoia.

YEAH, OK, SO LIKE PEOPLE HAVE THESE BOOKS, AND YOU KNOW LIKE THEY'RE SMALL BOOKS, BUT THEY'RE YOU KNOW, THICK, AND SO THEY'RE LIKE BIG, SO YOU KNOW THEY'RE BIG LITTLE BOOKS. And so, you know I think, you know, that's quite a concept. And so, you know, there might be some possibilities. You know. To do – something.

YEAH, SO WHAT'S IT ABOUT?

Oh, it's about this guy, you know, and he's living in this haunted house, and he sells it to this couple. And you know like they're haunted and stuff. It has really excellent special effects.

It's about being afraid of buying a house.

Exactly.

A door slammed shut behind him.

YOU KNOW, IT'S JUST LIKE I ALWAYS SAY WITH UNIONS. Now, they once had their place, you know, no one's going to deny that. But now, I mean you can't deny that when you look at industries that don't. You know, and it's the same with the Legion thing.

I MEAN, THERE WAS THIS ALLEGED INCIDENT, WITH THIS WOMAN, AND SHE SAID THAT THE MEN WERE STOPPING HER FROM GETTING TO THE WASHROOM, AND WHAT DID THEY DO? They bolted down the tables.

And in the same regard, oh yeah, well, you know, you look, you see, if you look at countries where there's more trade, more free enterprise, they're more democratic. The communist way, well, people tried that, didn't they, but it didn't work.

And if it didn't work, then there's no point in wishing for it, in dreaming for it. He waved his fingers by his head. Because it isn't practical. You know. That's fine. But you've got to be practical.

But you know, by the same token. I mean if you look at some of these jokers, these individuals who're politicians. You know sometimes I really wonder about that bunch.

HEY HEY, KIDDO, KIDDO, YOU WANT TO BE QUIET? Almost his bedtime. Yep. Isn't it? He held him upside down.

THEY HAD BEEN LYING TOGETHER FOR A WHILE AND WHEN SHE GOT UP SHE LOOKED BACK AT HER.

GOD, HE'S LIKE A TOTAL ASSHOLE.

Oh, totally.

God, but he looks alright, but if he's doing –

Oh yeah, I know. I mean he's like, first thing in morning, *breakfast, dude.* She popped open an imaginary beer can.

He thought about the cum on his face as he lay under her pussy.

HE LAY ON HIS BACK ON THE SOFA, AN ASHTRAY ON HIS CHEST.

OK HEDGES, HEDGES, WHAT IS IT ABOUT HEDGES. Hedges are edges, the edge, between places. Or they're like, no, they have to be clipped and they're clipped by old Italian men with moustaches or old Japanese men with bags under their eyes.

The house next door was a party house, with Melvins and LG-73 stickers on the front door. A couple people from the house were outside with a dog.

Their radio was on a Christian rock station.

Bob, would you and the Living Praise Choir lead us in "And to God be the glory"?

Hey. So how's it going?

Good, good, excellent.

Yeah, that was an excellent party.

Oh yeah, great.

Yeah, it wasn't bad, eh? At least it wasn't for the rent.

Oh yeah, you've had some of those?

No, not here, but where I used to live, yeah. But the guy, he couldn't get out enough people. So there was no point.

Yeah, if you don't have the money.

Oh sure.

Yeah, but that sure was a good party.

So that was a good evening.

Yeah. Quite the event.

I liked it a lot when, Jeff was pretty funny.

Oh yeah, of course, he's always like that. Yeah, he's got his act.

Receding hair line.

Receding hair line, flipping a nickel with his nipple. Used to work by weight but now he has to flick it.

So, you want to go up to Kingsway and then cut over?

Sure, whatever. When we get there.

No, we have to do it this way.

THEY WANDERED INTO THE KITCHEN. I'm getting hungry, how about you?

Oh yeah, anything around?

Just the thing. He pulled out two bowls, and put cold spaghetti and sauce in them, picking at the white strands with his fingers. Don't mind me. Just a sec. He punched the microwave. He had a glass of water while he waited for them to heat up.

OK, here we go, now it's just like you're a kid, and you're home for lunch in the wintertime.

So you know I was in the bar the other night, did I tell you what happened?

No.

Yeah, it was after work, you know, and I thought I'd go in after work and just grab a cold one. And, I don't know, I guess it was after seven or something because *Jeopardy* wasn't on and they were playing NTN.

Oh yeah?

Yeah, and so you know, I was just sitting there with a beer and some fries, so I didn't care, I started playing.

Yeah, how'd you do?

Oh great, I was smoking them. And the funny thing was, they didn't know who it was. That I was right there.

Why not?

Oh, cuz you know you have these codes, you just punch in these initials.

Oh great.

Oh yeah, it was excellent. Totally.

THEY WERE PLAYING POOL AT A BAR CALLED THE WATERFRONT'S EDGE.

So they called me in today.

Oh yeah, what for?

Speed.

Oh no.

Yeah, not up for it.

Oh drag.

Yeah, but the biggest drag was just acting like I cared.

Oh, I know that's the worst. You're just like, thinking, you stupid fuck, fuck you, and you have to smile and look.

Yeah, I mean can they think I actually care?

So, you gonna stick there?

Yeah, until I find something better.

Yeah, what're you gonna do.

THERE WAS FOUR OF THEM IN A DAISY CHAIN, TWO MEN AND TWO WOMEN.

HE WALKED INTO THE KITCHEN AND ASKED HER IF THEY HAD ANY. She took a bag out of the cupboard, standing on her toes to reach it.

THE THING IS, YOU DON'T WANT, WHAT YOU DON'T WANT IS FOR THE LAKE TO GIVE YOU AN ENEMA.

Yeah, no sense in that.

Oh, killer.

Now I've never had a problem with that, must have an unusually sensitive poop chute. But you know if you fall down, now in all likelihood.

Oh yeah, in all likelihood you're gonna catch a hoop ride.

Yeah well, you know, you never know, I'll try anything once. You never know, I might enjoy it.

Oh well, you can.

YEAH SO WHAT YOU WANT TO DO IS TO MAKE IT REALLY TIGHT. Good and tight.

Yeah, I've got it.

OK SO WHAT HAPPENS?

Yeah what happens is OK so first of all you have these girls, right?
And they used to be hookers. And they're, you know, making it,
doing whatever, but they get together or whatever and I don't know
about this part but they meet up with this guy, and he's like, he's
like a serial killer, right? And he's going to like torch the building or
whatever. Something about how he hires one of them as his, for a stud
party, or a stag, and you know a birthday cake, but he really puts it
into the oven. I don't know, maybe he works at a bakery, right? And
then, though, you know, he's not caught or whatever and so he joins
the army right, and goes over to, you know, Croatia. And meanwhile
he's like adopted this kid of one of the hookers he's killed, right, and
so it's cool, he's over there, and he sends his kid a My Dad was a
Peacekeeper in Croatia T-shirt. That's important later on, and when
he's over there, he meets this family of you know, Serbs or Croatians,
you know, whatever, and they've like got the scarves, and they just left
their fucking town and you know he has to protect them going through
all the buildings, you know with sniper fire and there's shelling all the
time. And one day he sees the guy, that guy, you know, who drives
around everywhere there, the president, Slobber Dan or whatever,
who got married, and our guy is a little psycho cuz he had to take
the little Serb or Croatian, whatever, kid to the hospital and it like
reminded him of his own kid back home. So he sees the guy and he
just like gets down there and fires off a round right, a couple shots,
but they don't get the guy they miss and hit a beautiful woman in the
face, and there's blood everywhere, and she was wearing a scarf and
sunglasses but you could still tell she was beautiful, and so he's like
totally depressed after this, and he's back at the camp, you know,
Friday night, and they're like goofing off for home videos, and he's
totally pissed off with himself for blowing a big opportunity. So he
like just like goes outside to let off a few rounds, but there's this kid
there, right, to sell some food from his village that was, you know,

like, totally shelled and everything, and he just like totally wastes the
kid, and everyone's running around, and no one knows who did it,
and he just goes to his room and tries to blow his head off, cuz, you
know, he's so totally depressed. But the thing is he doesn't, he doesn't
kill himself, you know, at the last minute some guy comes in to his
barracks, and the rifle moves and he just takes off his ear and part
of his neck, so he's comatose for a while, and they fly him back and
stuff and he kind of recovers, except that he has to be in a wheelchair,
right, but then he has to do something to make up for, you know,
being a serial killer and killing the wrong people in the war, so he
decides to start a, like a run or whatever, take his wheelchair like across
the country. And so the last thing is you see him with his kid in his
lap, using his one good hand to push the joystick on his wheelchair,
heading down the highway.

AND THEN THERE'S ANOTHER PART, I DON'T KNOW, LIKE A SEQUEL OR SOMETHING, PART TWO OR, BUT HE'S LIKE, I DON'T KNOW IF HE'S IN A WHEELCHAIR, PROBABLY NOT, MAYBE IT'S BEFORE, BUT NO, HE'S LIKE HE GETS MARRIED FINALLY, ONE OF THE HOOKERS, RIGHT, AND HE'S LIKE, THEY'RE MARRIED, ONE BIG HAPPY FAMILY, AND SHE'S LIKE COOKING AND DOING THE HOUSEWORK AND HE'S LIKE WHATEVER, AND EVERYONE'S HAPPY, BUT THEN HE FINDS OUT, YOU KNOW, WHAT SHE'S BEEN DOING. And he's like, he put that behind him, right, he's not like that anymore. And she just wants to drag him back.

OH YEAH, WELL, DID YOU HEAR? You heard, right? Yeah cuz he was arrested, eh? Yeah, cuz it was like the weirdest thing, you know, and everything. We, we went down to the 7-Eleven, you know, to get some smokes and chips and junk. And we're there, and like I go in and I get back out and he's like, there's these kids and they're just like yelling at him, you know, and I can't see what's going on. I mean, like there was a lots of kids there, you know I mean he's over at this car. Yeah, so like I'm just still trying to figure it out, you know, what was going on and so I go to this girl, you know, like what's going on, and she's like *what, do you like know this fucking* – and I'm like well, *you don't have to be ignorant*, you know, I mean, I didn't know what he was doing, if I had, I would've just, but you know and she's like *you stupid bitch* and I'm like *hey just shut up!* And then the cops get there and they like recognize me, right, I know them all from my you know whatever, I mean you know they used to pick me up and my little friends when we were wandering around drinking shit mix, you know like and so the cops're there and they push everyone around and the next thing I know is I see him there and his there's this stuff all over the front of his T-shirt? And his jeans? And his, and he's like, they push him to the ground, cuz you know he'd been, I don't know, and he's like *call my mom*, and so I went to the cop shop with him, and his mom gets there and she's just like evil eye, right, but then it's OK, used to it, whatever, and but I didn't see him after that, like I don't know.

Yeah, so he like marked Hornbus on it, right, in the dust on the back.

Yeah, and we're like, OK, let's go, and then but we turn this corner, and like stuff falls off the top, goes flying everywhere, and it's like my tapes, and I run out, to like get them, they're all over the road, and people are picking them up for me, and I throw them into my hat but they're like joking, oh yeah, not bad. You know, like talking about what the tapes are, all my mix tapes. Hilarious, eh, it's like it's your underwear and it's, or like when you try to empty garbage and Q-Tips just fall all over the place.

THEY WERE AT CHARLIE DON'T SURF, A RESTAURANT IN DOWNTOWN WHITE ROCK. Jeff was explaining the deal.

Yeah, and so like my brother's there, right, and they've got them there and it just seems like a natural, right? So I'm like, yeah, and I like meet up with them and they're like interested. So you know, I'm back here and I like get some money, you know, and well you know. So now –

The waitress brought their margaritas.

Yeah and so now, you know, they get into I have to go and pick the stuff up at, you know, up at PoCo, or PoMo, somewhere out there, you know, and like so now I –

So there wasn't really the –

No, so now like I'm, you know, I had all these problems with them, and like they're not there, or they were fine when they left. And I'm like left holding the bag and I'm just like, well I'm sorry.

Yeah.

Nothing I can do about it at this time. I mean, I was just trying to open up the North American market for you.

Their nachos arrived.

So you know what Jason's doing, eh?

No, what.

He's like, he's going to do one of those family books, you know.

YEAH, OK, AND SO LIKE HE PULLS OFF HIS GAUNCH AND WALKS INTO THE BATHROOM. There's enough light from outside. He looks at himself in the mirror, not smiling, runs his hand over his scalp. He opens the drawer and takes out deodorant, and rubs it in his pits. He puts the deodorant back, and opens his arms a couple of times, like a duck. He rubs his cock, looking at himself in the mirror. He squats a bit to separate his cheeks, and then walks out of the bathroom.

HE LOOKED AT THE GUY BENDING DOWN TO GET A *BUY AND SELL*.

Hey matador, what band?

Huh, the guy turned around.

Oh, Unsane, right on.

Yeah, they're pretty intense.

Saw them live, pretty –

Yeah they're pretty intense live –

Oh yeah they –

Yeah, but like their drummer, died of heroin.

Oh, no way.

Yeah, but like a year ago.

Oh no.

Oh, but I saw them.

Yeah, well, they got a new drummer.

Yeah, right.

Yeah they're pretty intense live.

Oh yeah.

Yeah, but I don't know if.

Yeah.

Yeah, this friend of mine had the disc. We were always over there so I heard it a lot.

Yeah.

And you know, I don't know. You know, spend the money. The guy walked over to the bank machine.

THE GUY WALKED UP THE HILL.

A DECK.

Yeah, we were thinking of a deck. You know, see.

That'd be nice.

Yeah, cuz you know, the thing is with your own place, you can like crank the tunes.

YEAH, CUZ YOU KNOW, I WAS SEEING THIS OTHER GIRL BEFORE. Oh yeah, I'd known her before, you know, from high school. We didn't really hang out in the same crowd, but anyway, she was like brutal. Yeah, no, it was, you know like she went through me like a pavement saw, just, you know, a clean cut.

YEAH, SO IT'S LIKE SUCK UP.

No, it isn't. You don't do that.

Yeah, no. Just stay pleasant.

You'll do fine.

Happy.

Happy.

YEAH, WELL YOU KNOW, CUZ IT'D BE STUPID TO SAY, YOU KNOW, TO TAKE, CUZ YOU KNOW LIKE THERE ISN'T A CHANCE.

AND I MEAN I KNOW THAT, BUT I CAN LIVE WITH THAT.

YEAH, WELL, YOU KNOW, THEY JUST CAN'T KEEP ASKING, TAKING. You know, cuz, there just isn't any money anymore. And so finally you've got to say no.

SHE LOOKED AT HIS EYEBROWS. He was frowning. Because you know like, whether it's a family, or you know the government, you know, or business, it's your same basic operating principle.

HE CARRIED THE ANSWERING MACHINE OUT TO THE GARBAGE CAN.

WALKING THROUGH THE SUBURBS, THE SONG WENT, *THEY'RE NOT EXACTLY LOVERS.*

Is it cocktail hour? She stuck her head out the kitchen door.

Yeah, sure.

He kept reading the paper. Read about Tyson. Jesus, that guy's amazing.

She brought out some drinks. He stirred his screwdriver with the mermaid swizzle stick.

Jesus, good vodka.

Yep, not bad.

Are we still on?

Oh yeah, we've barely cracked that puppy.

Yeah, it was a good deal?

Yep. No, it's worth it. She frowned to herself. Did we get?

What.

Did we – did – when did we get this?

What?

This.

Oh, on Thursday.

SEAN WAS HOME WHEN THEY GOT THERE, IN THE BACKYARD, MANEUVERING AROUND IN HIS POWER WHEELCHAIR LIKE A STUNT DOUBLE FROM *JAKE AND THE FATMAN*.

Hey. So how you guys doin'?

Hey. Not bad.

Yeah, so come on in.

So what've you been up to?

Oh, you know.

Yeah?

Usual. You know.

Yeah? Good. So.

Yeah, did some sketches.

Oh good, where are they?

Over on the picnic table. I was just looking at them.

Yeah, good. These are good. Yeah, good.

Oh, these are good.

So, like what's up with you guys?

Oh, you know.

Getting some work.

Yeah, and so like what've you got?

Oh, you mean like in terms of weed?

Yeah.

Well I've just got an eighth of pot left. And some hash, you can get a gram for fifteen.

Oh yeah, no, I think an eighth is good for us. Pot. What do you?

Yeah, no, I've got no interest in that right now.

Yeah.

Yeah so an eighth, that'll be forty-five.

What is it?

The usual. Yeah, I've been getting it pretty good. This is the first time I've been out for a while.

Yeah, oh, and we appreciate it. Totally.

Yeah?

Yeah, when you got back from Hornby and you were like, you'd saved that last eighth for us. Thanks.

Yeah, that was great.

Oh sure, well, you guys are regular, you know, I value my customers. Yeah, so it's forty-five. OK come by any time. He put the money in his hip pouch.

Clint Burnham is a Vancouver writer and teacher. Born in Comox, he lived in Toronto in the late 80s and early 90s, where he was a notorious player on the small press scene. He has lived in Vancouver since 1995, and has published two books of poetry (*Be Labour Reading* and *Buddyland*) and a collection of short stories (*Airborne Photo*). He has been attacked by audience members at readings of his work and students have protested the use of his writing in a college classroom. From 1999-2002 he ran a liberal arts outreach program in Vancouver's Downtown Eastside; he also teaches at Emily Carr Institute, and writes often on contemporary art.